Order this book online at www.trafford.com
or email orders@trafford.com

Most Trafford titles are also available at major online book retailers.

 www.trafford.com

North America & international
toll-free: 844 688 6899 (USA & Canada)
fax: 812 355 4082

Our mission is to efficiently provide the world's finest, most comprehensive book publishing service, enabling every author to experience success. To find out how to publish your book, your way, and have it available worldwide, visit us online at www.trafford.com

Because of the dynamic nature of the Internet, any web addresses or links contained in this book may have changed since publication and may no longer be valid. The views expressed in this work are solely those of the author and do not necessarily reflect the views of the publisher, and the publisher hereby disclaims any responsibility for them.

ISBN: 978-1-6987-1618-3 (sc)
ISBN: 978-1-6987-1619-0 (e)

Library of Congress Control Number: 2023924285

Print information available on the last page.

Trafford rev.   12/21/2023

The Adventures of

Spotty and Sunny

Book 10: A Fun Learning Series for kids

Author/ Pharmacist

Saisnath Baijoo

FAIRY MOTHER SITS ON THE HIGH FENCE. SHE SMILES. SHE FLIES DOWN. SHE LOOKS AROUND. SHE SEES EVERYONE IS HAVING FUN IN THE POOL. JORDI SEES MOTHER FAIRY. HE SCREAMS LOUDLY. HE IS HAPPY. EVERYONE LOOKS IN HIS DIRECTION.

HE SCREAMS LOUDLY. "LOOK. LOOK. MY FAIRY MOTHER CAME TO SEE ME."

CUDDLES BARKS AND STANDS ON HER BACK FEET. SHE RUNS TOWARDS HER IN JOY.

DOMINIC, JAS, DAVIN, SPOTTY, SUNNY AND DAVIN RUSHES TO HUG HER.

MOTHER FAIRY SAYS, "HELLO. I AM GLAD THAT YOU KIDS ARE HAVING SO MUCH FUN. THIS IS GREAT."

MOMS AND DADS RUSH TO HUG HER.

DAVIN AND DOMINIC PULLS HER ASIDE. DAVIN SAYS QUIETLY. "MOTHER FAIRY, OUR VACATIONS ARE ALL THE SAME. THEY ARE FUN AND YET SO BORING. HEY! CAN YOU SUGGEST SOMETHING A BIT DIFFERENT?"

JORDI RUNS TO HUG MOTHER FAIRY. HE NEARLY PUSHES HER IN THE SWIMMING POOL. SHE LIFTS JORDI. HE JOKES AND HUGS HER TIGHTLY. HE STRATCHES HIS HEAD AND JOKES, "FAIRY MOTHER. CAN YOU TAKE US SOMEWHERE LIKE MAYBE TO THE MOON?"

JAS POKES FUN AT JORDI, "OH! YES. TO THE MOON."

MANY PARENTS GATHER AROUND MOTHER FAIRY. SHE WHISPERS TO THE PARENTS. SHE THINKS FOR A MOMENT.

THEN SHE WALKS TO THE BORED
BUT FUN-LOVING KIDS.

MOTHER FAIRY SMILES, "NOW KIDS. CAN ANYONE
COUNT TO TWENTY AND THEN BACKWARDS?"

MR. SLO THUMPS HIS CHEST, "OH! YES. I
AM SLOW TO WALK BUT I CAN." HE TAKES
A DEEP BREATH AND SMILES.

"1, 2, 3, 4, 5, 6,7, 8, 9, 10, 11, 12, 13, 14, 15, 16, 17, 18, 19, 20."

SUNNY JUMPS UP AND DOWN. SHE DOES THE
MOON DANCE, "I AM VERY FAST. NOW. IT IS MY
TURN TO COUNT BACKWARDS. OH YES! I CAN
DO IT WITH MY EYES CLOSED. HERE GOES. 20,
19, 18, 17, 16, 15, 14, 13, 12, 11, 10, 9, 8, 7, 6, 5, 4, 3, 2, 1."

EVERYONE CLAPS. BIG RED DANCES WITH JOY.

MOTHER FAIRY JOKES, "GOOD JOB. I AM NOT FINISHED YET. NOW. 20 PLUS 10 AND MINUS 5."

SPOTTY JUMPS UP AND DOWN, " I KNOW. I KNOW THE ANSWER IS SWEET 25.

MOTHER FAIRY FLIES TO THE PARENTS. SHE WHISPERS TO THEM. EVERYONE DANCES WITH JOY. THEY ARE HAPPY.

MOTHER FAIRY FLIES TO THE KIDS, "WELL.
MY LOVES. 25 PEOPLE CAN GO ON MY
PLANE. THAT IS INCLUDING CUDDLES."

MISS PELICAN COUNTS VERY FAST. "1, 2, 3, 4, 5,
6,7, 8, 9, 10, 11, 12, 13, 14, 15, 16,17, 18, 19, 20, 21, 22, 23,
24, 25. BUT THERE IS ONLY 21 PEOPLE HERE?

MOTHER FAIRY SMILES, "OH YES. WELL. WE NEED TWO
PILOTS AND TWO FLIGHT ATTENDANTS TO SERVE FOOD
AND VIDEO GAMES. YOU KIDS WILL BE VERY HUNGRY."

JOSE ADDS WITH HIS FINGERS, "WELL
21 PLUS 2 PLUS 2 IS 25."

MOM, DAD, SUNNY PARENTS, BIG RED FAMILY, JOSE
FAMILY, MISS SNAPPER, MR AND MRS. SLO, DR. IGUANA
AND MISS PELICAN ARE HAPPY TO GO ANYWHERE

SPOTTY ADDS, 20 PLUS 10 MINUS 5 EQUAL 25.

JOSE ADDS 21 PLUS 2 PLUS 2 EQUAL 25.

THE NEXT DAY, EVERYONE IS AT THE EVERGLADES AIRPORT WAITING TO GO ON MOTHER FAIRY'S PLANE.

"BUT WHERE ARE WE GOING DAD?" JAS SAYS.

DAD ANSWERS, "OH! NO ONE KNOWS. IT IS A BIG SURPRISE. I KNOW IT IS A LONG RIDE."

"WOW. OUR PRIVATE PLANE. NOW THAT IS COOL." DAVIN SAYS.

WHILE ON BOARD, THE CHILDREN LOOKS SAD AS THE FLIGHT ATTENDANT GIVES EVERYONE ADDITION AND SUBTRACTION BOOKS. SHE SMILES AND SAYS, "KIDS REMEMBER READING IS FUN AND LEARNING IS FUN."

JAS JOKES WITH A SAD FACE, "ARE WE IN SCHOOL ON OUR SUMMER BREAK?"

AFTER THE KIDS COMPLETE THEIR SCHOOL
WORK, HAPPY FACES RETURN. THEY PLAY
VIDEO GAMES ON THEIR COMPUTERS. NO ONE
IS SLEEPING OR TIRED. THEY ASK THE FLIGHT
ATTENDANTS REGULARLY TWO QUESTIONS.

"WHERE ARE WE GOING OR ARE WE THERE YET?"

SHE SMILES ONLY.

AFTER MANY HOURS OF FLYING, THE PILOT ANNOUNCE,
"IS EVERYONE HAVING A WONDERUL TIME? WE ARE
NEARING OUR DESTINATION. REMEMBER, ALWAYS
FASTEN YOUR SEATBELTS WHETHER YOU ARE IN A
CAR OR IN A PLANE. YOUR SAFETY COMES FIRST."

SUDDENLY LIKE MAGIC, EVERYONE IS STARING AT INDIA'S ROVER ON THE SOUTH SIDE OF THE MOON. MOTHER FAIRY SAYS," WE ARE NOW AT INDIA'S MISSION CONTROL ROOM IN THE VISITORS' AREA." EVERYONE CLAPS.

"I FEEL THAT WE ARE ON THE MOON. I CAN TOUCH IT." MOM SCREAMS WITH JOY.

"AWW. IT IS SO BEAUTIFUL AND YET SO PEACEFUL." BIG RED SAYS TO HIS CHILDREN.

"THE MOON ROVER IS ON MY NORTH SIDE." SCREAMS DAD IN JOY.

"NOT REALLY. IT IS ON MY EAST SIDE." SAYS DOMINIC.

"AWW MAN. IT'S ON MY WEST SIDE." MR. SLO, OUR TURTLE SAYS SLOWLY.

MISS CAN ADDS, "NOW, I AM SEEING THE ROVER MOON LANDING LIVE. IT IS REALLY ON MY SOUTH SIDE."

MR. TAM SHAKES HIS TAMBORINE WITH TEARS IN HIS EYES, "THIS IS A HISTORIC DAY IN FRONT OF MY EYES."

"THEN, I MUST BE DREAMING. ARE WE ALL DREAMING? I FEEL THAT I CAN TOUCH THE ROVER." SUNNY SAYS.

"WE ARE SO CLOSE TO THE MOON. I LOOK AT IT EVERY NIGHT." SPOTTY SAYS HAPPILY.

AFTER MANY HOURS LOOKING AT THE MOON, IT DISAPPEARS LIKE A SPECK OF DUST FAR, FAR AWAY. EVERYONE IS HAPPY BUT ALSO SAD.

OUR PILOT SAYS, " FRIENDS, IF YOU LOOK ON YOUR LEFT OR RIGHT WINDOW YOU WILL SEE THE TAJ MAHAL."

LEFT

RIGHT

17

DR. IGUANA SAYS, "KIDS. IT IS ONE OF
THE WONDERS OF THE WORLD."

MOM SAY, "THERE IS A LOVE STORY
BEHIND THE TAJ MAHAL."

THE PILOT SAYS AGAIN, "FRIENDS, OUR MOTHER
FAIRY HAS REQUESTED ANOTHER SPECIAL
TREAT JUST FOR YOU ALL. ANYONE WOULD
LIKE TO SEE THE STATUE OF LIBERTY?"

EVERYONE CLAPS AND SINGS AS THE PILOT
FINISHES SPEAKING. EVERYONE IS HAPPY.

AFTER A FEW MINUTES THE PILOT COMES BACK
ON THE SPEAKER AGAIN, "KIDS, LOOK OUTSIDE
YOUR WINDOWS. TO YOUR LEFT AND RIGHT
YOU WILL SEE THE STATUE OF LIBERTY."

"IT IS SO BEAUTIFUL. I FLY HERE EVERY
YEAR." MISS PELICAN SAYS.

SPOTTY ADDS, "ONE DAY SOON, WE WILL VISIT NEW YORK. I WANT TO TOUCH THE STATUE OF LIBERTY."

SUNNY HOLDS SPOTTY'S HANDS,
"BROTHER, CAN I COME WITH YOU?"

SPOTTY SAYS, "YES, FOR SURE. TOMORROW. IT IS SCHOOL TIME AGAIN. I DON'T WANT TO MISS ANY DAYS OF SCHOOL. I AM AN HONOR STUDENT."

SUNNY SAYS TO SPOTTY, "BROTHER. WE ARE HONOR STUDENTS. I LOVE MY SCHOOL TIME. REMEMBER READING IS FUN. LEARNING IS FUN. I AM GLAD TO GO BACK TO SCHOOL."

OUR JOURNEY ENDS BUT THERE IS MORE FUN AND LEARNING ADVENTURE CONTINUES.

Printed in the United States
by Baker & Taylor Publisher Services